On the Move

Mass Migrations

by Scotti Cohn

illustrated by Susan Detwiler

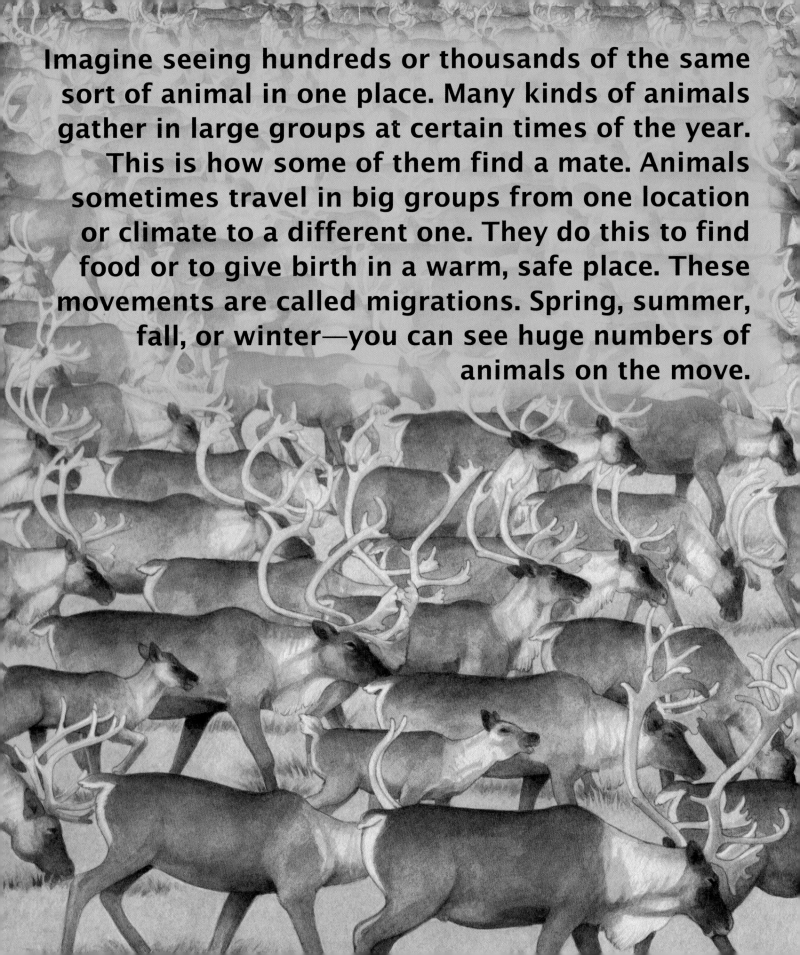

Imagine seeing hundreds or thousands of the same sort of animal in one place. Many kinds of animals gather in large groups at certain times of the year. This is how some of them find a mate. Animals sometimes travel in big groups from one location or climate to a different one. They do this to find food or to give birth in a warm, safe place. These movements are called migrations. Spring, summer, fall, or winter—you can see huge numbers of animals on the move.

Spring paints the forest in fresh shades of purple, yellow, and green. Warm rain falls in drips and drops on the cold ground. Spotted salamanders crawl out of their underground homes after dark. The earth is soft and cool beneath their feet. The salamanders are ready to go. This is their big night, and soon they are on the move. They wiggle through the woods. They squiggle across the fields. They wriggle across the roads. Finally, they reach the wetland pool. There they find their mates. Females lay their eggs just under the surface of the water.

Spring swoops onto the prairie on a brisk, bold breeze. A warbling, trumpeting, chirping noise gets louder and louder. Soon hundreds of thousands of sandhill cranes fill the sky. They're on the move!

When you look at the cranes flying, they look tiny. Once they are on the ground, you can see that some of them are taller than you.

During spring migration, they court each other by doing what looks like a dance. They flap their wings, bow their heads, run, skip, and leap.

Thousands of horseshoe crabs are on the move in the spring. They look like little armored tanks with spiked tails. They scuttle out of the bay onto the beach to mate. The females lay eggs in the sand.

Red knots fly in to eat the eggs. The birds are tired and thin after their long trip from South America. Soon they will be plump and ready to fly to the Arctic to nest.

Common green darner dragonflies hover over nearby gardens and fields. They are on their way north. Larger groups of them will pass through here when they fly south in the fall.

The bright summer sun shines all day and all night in the far north. A mother caribou snorts and shakes her head. She is telling her calf to stay close to her. He is still too small to protect himself against bears and wolves.

Thousands of caribou travel north every spring. Calves are born where many tender young plants grow. The caribou have plenty to eat there. By mid-summer, the herd is again on the move. They travel up into the mountains. Cool mountain breezes help keep mosquitoes away from them.

Thousands of chimney swifts are on the move in late summer and early fall. Each evening they soar and swoop above an old brick smokestack. They dip and dive. They chitter and chatter like children on a playground. Around and around they fly. Then they swirl down into the smokestack to spend the night. They are getting ready to travel south for the winter. Most of them will be gone by the end of October.

The end of summer is near. Crickets are singing their evening song. Deep in a cave, a Brazilian free-tailed bat pup wakes up and flexes her wings. She has been roosting all day and now she's hungry. She's not the only one. Soon huge clouds of small, dark, winged bodies whirl through the sky. The bats are hunting for moths, beetles, and other insects. For the first time in her life, the new pup joins her mother to look for food. In the fall, she and the rest of her colony will be on the move, migrating south for the winter.

Up north, the autumn air is chilly. Monarch butterflies flutter their brilliant orange and gold wings. Soon they are on the move. More and more monarchs join the flight until tens of millions of monarchs are flying south together.

These butterflies have not made this trip before. Somehow they know to take the same route as the monarchs who lived before them. They even stop to rest in the same places. Once they reach their southern home, the monarchs will sleep for much of the winter.

Where polar bears live, fall brings a cruel chill to the air. Days grow short, and snow clouds fill the sky. On huge padded feet, the polar bears lumber toward the water's edge. They have been on land for several months. When they are on land, they eat only berries, roots, bird eggs, and small animals. The bears are very hungry now. They test the ice that forms on the surface of the water. Once it is frozen solid, they're on the move. They travel across the ice to catch seals.

It's the end of a sunny autumn day in the forest. Gold, orange, and red leaves flutter in the trees. More leaves cover the ground. A soft rustling sound comes from the base of an oak. A cottonmouth snake is on the move. As the cool evening passes, many kinds of snakes slip, slide, and slither through the dry leaves. Every year at this time, snakes that live in cold climates travel to dens to spend the winter. They often return to the same den each year, and large groups of snakes may share the same den.

Most of the year, northern elephant seals live alone. They swim, dive, and hunt. Come winter, they are on the move. They haul out on land, and soon the beach is covered with seals. They squawk, squeak, bellow, belch, grunt, and gurgle. Mature males battle each other to prove their strength. Pregnant females give birth. Come summer, the seals are back on land to shed old skin and hair, replacing it with new (molt). Elephant seals do not need to eat while they're on land. They have a lot of fat, called blubber, stored on their bodies.

Summer, fall, and winter, salmon are on the move! They swim from the ocean upstream to the place where they were born. It's hard work. The salmon leap and splash as they struggle against the current. They do not eat along the way. When they finally reach their spawning ground, they are worn out and weak.

Overhead large numbers of bald eagles wheel through the sky. Many of the eagles live in the area year-round. Come winter, some travel from a frozen world where there isn't enough food. They are all eager to feast on salmon.

Out in the ocean, thousands of gray whales are on the move. They swim slowly and steadily south for the winter to warm lagoons to give birth to their calves. The whales travel thousands of miles. They swim all day and all night for three months. Once they reach the lagoons, the whales do not find much to eat. They live on the fat stored in their bodies. In the spring, they travel with their calves to northern waters. There they feed on small shrimp-like animals (amphipods) from the bottom of the ocean floor.

For Creative Minds

Animal Migrations: What, When, Where, and Why?

Most people think about birds migrating in the spring and fall because huge flocks of birds are so visible in many areas. But birds are not the only animals that migrate. Some mammals, reptiles, fish, birds, amphibians, and even some invertebrates migrate. Many mammals and birds learn the migration route from their parents while others travel only by instinct. Scientists don't understand how animals know when and where to travel.

Some animals follow food sources or protection from seasonal weather. They often travel the same routes year after year and may even return to the same tree or nesting area as their parents and grandparents before them.

Some animals migrate as part of their life cycles. Animals that live alone most of the time (solitary) will often gather in large numbers at predictable places at predictable times of the year in order to find mates. Other animals travel to specific locations to lay eggs or to give birth and raise young before returning to their "normal" territory.

Animals may migrate year after year, or once in their lifetime.

Migrations can be long distances (for example, from tropical areas around the equator to the poles) or just a few hundred miles. Some might only travel up or down a mountain.

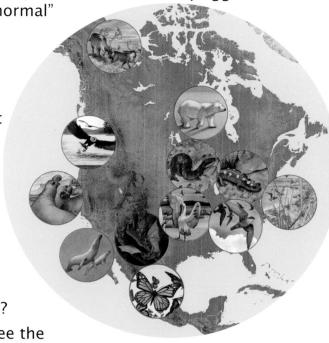

All of the animals mentioned in this book gather in predictable locations at predictable times of the year—right here in North America. You can go to these locations to see the animals.

Use the information in the next few pages to answer these questions:

1. Which animal gathering is closest to where you live?

2. What month or season would you best be able to see the animals?

3. How many animals could you see in one day?

4. Which animals are mammals, reptiles, fish, birds, amphibians, or invertebrates?

Brazilian free-tailed bats fly north to Texas, Arizona, and New Mexico in the spring. Females give birth to pups in June. The pups start to fly in August. Look for thousands of bats in August and September as these mammals leave their roosts at dusk. When the weather cools, the bats fly south to where there are still plenty of insects to eat.

Between 500 and 1,000 polar bears gather near Churchill, Manitoba, Canada each fall. They wait for the Hudson Bay to ice over. Once the bay freezes, these mammals scatter on the ice to hunt seals and whales through the winter. As the ice thaws in the spring, the bears ride the ice floes back to land. They'll spend the summer looking for whatever food they can find—even plants.

On the first warm, rainy night of spring in New England, salamanders travel to small ponds to breed. Hundreds of these amphibians gather to find mates. They will cross roads or crawl over anything in their way to get to the same ponds where they may have been born.

Salmon are born in freshwater but spend much of their lives in the ocean. As adults, these fish will return to the freshwater in which they were born. Depending on the location and the salmon species, you might see hundreds or hundreds of thousands of salmon swimming up-current in the summer, fall, or winter so they can breed and lay eggs. Salmon live in both the Pacific and Atlantic Oceans and now some even live in the Great Lakes.

Not all bald eagles migrate. If these birds live in areas where the water freezes during the winter, they will migrate to follow food sources. You might see a few or a few hundred eagles hunting salmon as the fish swim toward their breeding grounds. Fish trapped by the locks or dams also make for easy hunting. You can often find eagles around locks and dams on some large rivers.

Once a year, horseshoe crabs gather on beaches to breed. The females lay their eggs in the sand near the high tide line. Around the new and full moons in late May and early June, you can see millions of these invertebrates on the beaches around the Delaware Bay. You can also see them on other beaches up and down the Atlantic coast.

Adult red knots fly between South America and the Arctic every year. These tiny birds arrive on the shores of the Delaware Bay, just as the horseshoe crabs are laying eggs in the spring. They eat their fill of horseshoe crab eggs. After a short rest, they fly the rest of the way to their summer nesting grounds in the Arctic.

Chimney swifts lay eggs and raise young in eastern North America in the summer. Come fall, these birds gather by the thousands, getting ready to migrate. Look for the flocks around chimneys and other tall structures. They'll fly to the rainforests of South America for the winter. Not only are the rainforests warm, but there's lots of food there.

Hundreds of northern elephant seals gather twice a year at rookeries along the Pacific coastline from Alaska south to Baja California. In the late spring and early summer, these mammals come ashore to molt. They gather in winter to give birth and find a mate. They don't eat while on land but hunt fish once they are back in the water.

Hundreds of thousands of sandhill cranes gather at the Platte River in Nebraska in the spring. They eat and rest for up to a month before separating and flying further north to their summer nesting grounds. As cold weather approaches in the fall, the birds fly south looking for a ready supply of insects and seeds to eat.

Monarch butterflies migrate to warm weather for the winter. When they wake in the spring, they fly north to find the food they need to eat and plants they need to lay eggs. Look for these insects (invertebrates) in Mexico, coastal California, Texas, and Florida in the winter.

Gray whales leave their summer feeding grounds in Alaska as the weather starts to turn cold. They swim south towards warmer waters to breed and give birth. Because these huge mammals swim close to shore, you can sometimes see them from land on their swim south in the fall or back north in the spring. Look for them in their winter birthing and breeding grounds around Baja California and the Sea of Cortez.

Snakes need to protect themselves from cold weather. At the Shawnee National Forest in southern Illinois, many snakes migrate short distances to winter dens in the cracks and crevices of limestone bluffs. The reptiles gather into large balls for warmth and hibernate through the winter. Come spring and fall, you might spot up to 30 snakes in an afternoon crossing the road to or from their winter dens.

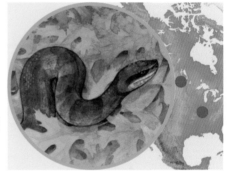

Caribou herds leave the forests in the spring and migrate to tundra meadows in Alaska and Northern Canada. Caribou young are born as soon as the snow melts. There's lots of food in the meadows and not too many predators. This gives the young mammals a chance to grow big and strong. They spend the winter in the forest where it's easier for them to find food.

1, 2, & 3 Answers will vary. For links and information on specific locations to see animals, go to the related websites on the book's homepage at ArbordalePublishing.com.

4: Mammals: Mexican free-tailed bats, polar bears, elephant seals, gray whales, caribou. Reptiles: snakes. Fish: salmon. Birds: eagles, chimney swifts, sandhill cranes. Amphibians: salamanders. Invertebrates: Monarch butterflies, horseshoe crabs.

For Laiken, who is always on the move!—SC

To Jon with gratitude for his support and encouragement—SD

Thanks to the following animal experts for verifying the accuracy of the information in this book:

· Brazilian free-tailed bats: Pam Cox, Supervisory Park Ranger, Division of Interpretation, Carlsbad Caverns National Park

· caribou: Cathy Curby, Wildlife Interpretive Specialist, Arctic National Wildlife Refuge

· chimney swifts: Georgean and Paul Kyle, Project Directors, Driftwood Wildlife Association

· elephant seals: Joan Crowder, Docent, Friends of Elephant Seals

· gray whales: Jason Richards, Chief of Interpretation and Education; Kaye London, Associate Wildlife Biologist; and Benjamin Pister at Cabrillo National Monument

· green darner dragonfly: Celeste Mazzacano, Project Coordinator, Migratory Dragonfly Partnership

· horseshoe crabs and red knots: Ronald L. Ohrel Jr., Director, Marine Public Education Office, Delaware Sea Grant and Stewart Michels, Delaware Division of Fish and Wildlife

· polar bears: Steve Selden, Expedition Leader, and Ted Martens, Sustainability Director, Natural Habitat Adventures

· salamanders: Patti Smith, Naturalist, Bonnyvale Environmental Education Center

· salmon and bald eagles: Joe Meehan, Lands and Refuge Program Coordinator, Alaska Department of Fish and Game and Charles Gibilisco, Community Outreach Environment Education Specialist, Washington Department of Fish and Wildlife

· sandhill cranes: Keanna Leonard, Education Director, Iain Nicolson Audubon Center at Rowe Sanctuary

· snakes: Chad Deaton, Wildlife Biologist, Shawnee National Forest, U.S. Forest Service

Library of Congress Cataloging-in-Publication Data

Cohn, Scotti, 1950-
  On the move : seasonal migrations / by Scotti Cohn ; illustrated by Susan Detwiler.
    pages cm
  Audience: Ages 4-9.
  ISBN 978-1-60718-616-8 (English hardcover) -- ISBN 978-1-60718-628-1 (English pbk.) -- ISBN 978-1-60718-640-3 (English ebook (downloadable)) 1. Animal migration--Juvenile literature. I. Detwiler, Susan, illustrator. II. Title.
  QL754.C635 2013
  591.56'8--dc23
                          2012034470

Also available in Spanish: Avanzando . . . de aquí para allá: migraciones masivas, translated by Rosalyna Toth 978-1-60718-712-7   Spanish hardcover ISBN 978-1-60718-652-6   Spanish eBook downloadable ISBN 978-1-60718-664-9   Interactive, read-aloud eBook featuring selectable English and Spanish text and audio (web and iPad/tablet based) ISBN

Interest level: 004-009   Lexile® Level: 690L
key phrases for educators: life cycles, migration, seasons; FCM: map, animal classification

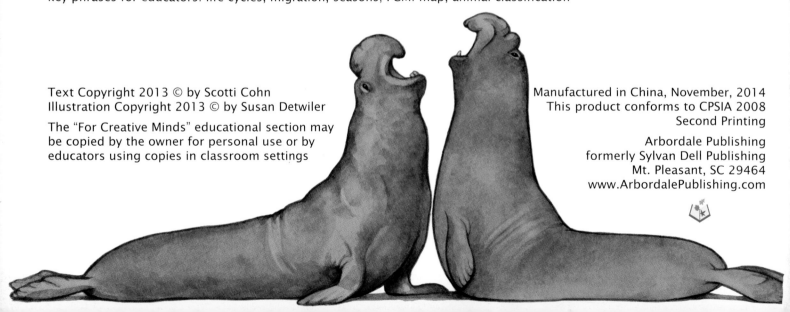

Manufactured in China, November, 2014
This product conforms to CPSIA 2008
Second Printing

Arbordale Publishing
formerly Sylvan Dell Publishing
Mt. Pleasant, SC 29464
www.ArbordalePublishing.com